Biscuit visits the doctor /

E Cap

149203

Capucilli, Alyssa Satin.

C WDC			

Biscuit
Visits the Doctor

For the wonderful veterinarians
who keep pets healthy . . . everywhere!
—A.S.C

by Alyssa Satin Capucilli

HarperFestival®
A Division of HarperCollinsPublishers

Based on the illustration style of Pat Schories
Interior illustrations by Rose Mary Berlin
Biscuit Visits the Doctor
Text copyright © 2008 by Alyssa Satin Capucilli. Illustrations copyright © 2008 by Pat Schories.
HarperCollins®, ≝®, and HarperFestival® are trademarks of HarperCollins Publishers. Printed in the United States of America. All rights reserved.
For information address HarperCollins Children's Books, a division of HarperCollins Publishers. 1350 Avenue of the Americas, New York, NY 10019.
www.harpercollinschildrens.com
Library of Congress catalog card number: 2008924823
ISBN 978-0-06-112843-1

"Come along, Biscuit.
We're going to visit Dr. Green.
It's time for your checkup!"
Woof, woof!

"Dr. Green is a veterinarian, Biscuit.
She cares for many different animals.
Dr. Green makes sure they are all healthy and strong."
Woof, woof!

"There are bunnies and gerbils. . . ."

Squawk! Squawk!
Woof, woof!

"And you found a parrot, Biscuit!"
Woof!

"Here comes Dr. Green."
Woof, woof!

"Are you ready, Biscuit?
It's our turn now."
Woof!

"First, Dr. Green will weigh and measure you, Biscuit.
Let's see how much you've grown!"
Woof, woof!

"Funny puppy! No tugging."
Woof!

"Dr. Green will look at your paws.
She'll listen to your heartbeat, too."
Woof, woof! Woof, woof!

"Shhh! Quiet, Biscuit!"

"Sit, Biscuit, sit.
Dr. Green will check your eyes and your ears."
Woof!

"She can even check your teeth. Open wide, Biscuit!
That's the way!"
Woof, woof!

"You must hold still when
Dr. Green gives you a shot, Biscuit.
She wants you to stay healthy and strong, too.
That wasn't so bad, was it?"
Woof, woof!

"Oh, no, Biscuit!
It's not time to roll over now!"
Woof!
"Silly puppy!"

"You did a great job, Biscuit.
Dr. Green has a special treat just for you."
Woof, woof!

"And you have a special treat for Dr. Green.
It's a big kiss!"
Woof, woof!

"Come along, Biscuit.
It's time to go home."
Woof, woof!
"Wait, Biscuit.

What have you found now?"

Woof, woof!
"Sweet puppy.
There are three little kittens."

Mew! Mew! Mew!
Woof!

"Off we go, Biscuit.
It was fun to visit with our friend Dr. Green."
Woof, woof!
"And meet some new friends, too!"
Woof!